THE LOST CHRISTMAS TOYS

Written & Illustrated by John Patience

It was Christmas Eve. The sleigh was loaded and Santa was carrying out his sack. Another moment and he would have been gone.
Suddenly a couple of elves ran out from the Magic Grotto carrying a teddy and a doll.

"Wait!" they shouted, pulling at Santa's red coat and dancing around him. "You've forgotten these!"

"Goodness me. I'd forget my beard if it were loose," chuckled Santa.
He took the teddy and the little doll and sat them on the sleigh with the other toys. Then with a "Giddy up, Rudolf," and a wave to the helpful elves, away he flew.

At first Teddy and Dolly enjoyed the ride on Santa's sleigh. It was wonderful to be flying so high in the night sky. Then the air began to turn cold. The North Wind sprang up and soon it was blowing a blizzard. Now the sleigh ride was very rough. Dolly and Teddy bounced around helplessly. They tried their very best to hold on, but the wind caught hold of them and blew them away. Dolly and Teddy fell head over heels, down through the swirling snowflakes.

The toys landed in a deep, soft snowdrift. They struggled out and began to wander around in the woods, not knowing quite what to do. A little mouse poked her head out from a doorway in the roots of a tree.

"Come inside before you freeze to death, you silly things!" she squeaked.

Teddy and Dolly did as they were told and were soon sitting by a warm fireside drinking hot cocoa and eating buttered muffins.

"We must be presents for some little boy or girl," said Teddy, "but I don't know how we're ever going to find them."

"I think I know someone who can help," said Mrs Mouse.

Mrs Mouse led the toys up a winding stairway to a room at the top of the tree, where she introduced them to Mr Owl. Mr Owl listened to Dolly and Teddy's story. Then he put on his glasses and looked carefully at the labels which were tied around the toys' necks.

"These are gift tags," said Owl. "They say 'Merry Christmas to Sophie'."

"Sophie must be a little girl and I imagine she must live in the town over there," said Mrs Mouse. She pointed out through the window to where Teddy and Dolly could see lots of distant, twinkling lights.

"Tomorrow morning is
Christmas morning," said Dolly.
"We must find Sophie by then.
We can't disappoint her."
Owl led Teddy and Dolly out on to
his balcony.

"Climb on to my back," he said.
"I'll fly you to town."
Dolly and Teddy looked at each
other a little doubtfully, but they
did as Owl suggested. Owl spread
his wings and launched himself
into the air.

Before long, Owl was flying low over the roof-tops of the town. He swooped down towards the park where a snowman was standing by a big Christmas tree.

"This is General Frosty," said Owl.

"At your service," said General Frosty, saluting smartly.
Owl quickly explained the situation and General Frosty nodded.

"No problem," he said. "I'll summon up the troops."
General Frosty lifted his bugle and blew loudly.

Then, from north, south, east and west, lots of snowmen came running across the park. They formed a line in front of General Frosty and saluted.

"Very good, men," said the General. "Now, pay attention! Which one of you was made by a little girl named Sophie?"

A jolly-looking snowman in a brown felt hat stepped forward.

"I was," he said.

"Excellent," said General Frosty. "Dolly and Teddy are Sophie's lost Christmas presents. Please take them to her."

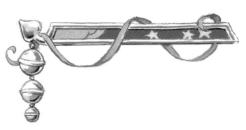

Sophie's snowman picked up Dolly and Teddy and ran with them through the streets of the town. He arrived at Sophie's house just as the sun was rising. It was Christmas Day! The snowman took off his scarf and wrapped it around Teddy and Dolly to keep them warm. He placed the toys on Sophie's doorstep and this was where she found them later in the day.

"They're lovely," said Sophie, picking up the toys and hugging them, "but I wonder why Santa didn't leave them in the house with my other presents?"